D1490402

SPECIAL AND DIFFERENT

THE AUTISM TRAVELER

Volume 1

THE BEGINNING OF THE AUTISM ADVENTURE

ISBN 978-1-64079-667-6 (Paperback)
ISBN 978-1-64079-668-3 (Digital)

Copyright © 2017 by Steven Tomasino
All rights reserved. No part of this publication may be reproduced, distributed, or transmitted in any form or by any means, including photocopying, recording, or other electronic or mechanical methods without the prior written permission of the publisher. For permission requests, solicit the publisher via the address below.

Christian Faith Publishing, Inc.
296 Chestnut Street
Meadville, PA 16335
www.christianfaithpublishing.com

Printed in the United States of America

THE BEGINNING OF THE AUTISM ADVENTURE

Stories taken from
The Holy Bible

As Told and Illustrated
by Steven Tomasino

INTRODUCTION

Hi I'm Steven Tomasino. I'm autistic, and I love Bible stories. The following stories include me walking through Bible times. I hope you enjoy them.

Once upon a time in a faraway land, there lived a young man named Steve who lived all by himself without anyone else at all "*Ah! This is the life!*" said Steve, happy and peaceful as can be, lying on a hammock with his soda. Unlike other grown-up men, what he always does is hang around the house doing whatever he wants like draw pictures and watch movies. Because Steve is autistic.

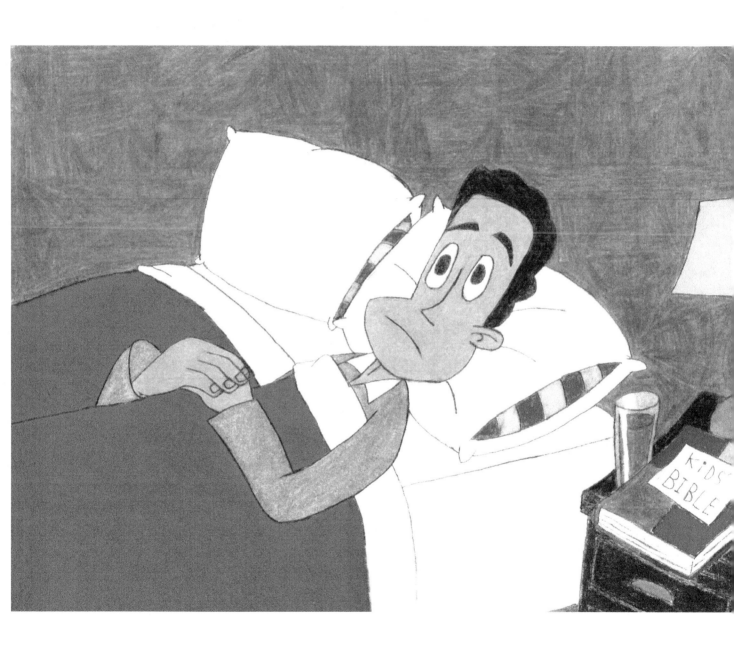

Although Steve cleans around the house a little bit, he is sometimes lazy, prideful, and even a little bit lonely. Steve went to bed that night, wondering, "*Am I really that special?*" Most of all, Steve feels different than any other adults, because after all, Steve is autistic.

Then the next day, Steve decided to go for a walk. "I guess I'll give this beautiful day a chance…for a little workout," said Steve to himself. So he left the house locked up and on the trails into the woods while listening to his iPod.

Walking alone in the woods with his walking stick, talking to himself, Steve stopped next to the big tree for a moment.  "Hey there, buttercup! You working out?" said Steve as the butterfly landed above his walking stick. Then all of a sudden, Steve noticed something loose; the ground he was standing on was beginning to crack. Because as he stomped his walking stick twice, he fell into the hole, deep down underground, where the historical Bible Chamber was. "Oh man!" said Steve "I wonder how long that old room been down here!"

Exploring the old room, Steve looked around the hall-way filled with hieroglyphic stories from the Bible. The only object he spotted was a single book on a table in the middle of the room. But it wasn't just an ordinary book. It hap-pened to be the Ultimate Book of Life.

As Steve opened it, flipping some dusty pages, Steve sneezed. Suddenly the por-tal door began to open. Steve found himself trapped. Steve felt himself being lifted and carried through time until he landed in the historical world of the Bible.

Genesis

Chapter 1

Steve was so surprised to find himself in a place known as the Garden of Eden, found in Genesis, the first book of the Bible. "Where am I now?" said Steve to himself.

Wondering in the garden, Steve met two naked people, Adam and Eve. "Hello there," said Adam. He asked, "What name do we call you?"

"Oh I'm, uh...Steve!" answered Steve, with a shock and nervous look of how they both looked naked. "I'm autistic who is way different as you two guys are!"

"I say we're special the way God made us!" said Eve. "And everything we have here in this garden is perfect!"

Adam showed Steve the rest of the garden. Like the Four Rivers of the Pishon, the Gihon, the Tigris, and Euphrates. Even the animals that Adam named weren't always wild. "I wonder if there any dinosaurs around here," said Steve. Later, he joined Adam and Eve in the hot spring with a little conversation for a while. "Ah! I can get used to this Animal Kingdom," said Steve, enjoying himself. He felt a crush on Eve, but he knew she was married to Adam. They both also told Steve about two trees in the middle of the garden.

"That tree over there is the tree of life," said Eve. "We may eat from it and live in Paradise forever."

"And the other tree on that side is the tree of knowl-edge of good and evil!" said Adam. "Which we are not allowed to eat. For if we do, we will die."

"Well, if there's only one rule around here, just go along with it!" agreed Steve. Nearby, lurking in the trees, a crafty old serpent kept an eye on Adam and Eve in every moment. For this serpent was more clever than any other wild animal that the Lord had made.

"S–s–soon they shall s–s–see things–s–s in my way. . . with a little s–s–snack!" said the serpent in every sinister word.

Steve had never spent the night in the historical nature like the Garden of Eden before. Then the next day in the afternoon, while Eve was alone, a crafty old serpent appeared to her and said with a sinister smile, "Dear child! Why mus-s-st you not eat the fruit of any trees-s-s that is-s in the middle of the garden?"

Eve said to the serpent what she remembered, "We may eat the fruit of trees of the garden, but not of the tree of knowledge. We will die if we eat from it."

"You can only s–s–seee that you surely will not die!" The serpent said, "God knows–s–s that when you eat the fruit of the tree, your eyes–s–s will be opened, and you will be like God knowing the difference between good and evil. S–s–so go on! Tas–s–ste it! Have a bite!" As Eve looked at the fruit of the tree that was good to eat, she felt like it would make one person wise. So she took some of the fruit and ate it. And now, when Adam came to her, she also gave some to him, and he ate it. Meanwhile, Steve was trying to pick some fruit from the tree of life. Because he thought that if he took a bite of it, he might be strong and super healthy for all time. But it was too late when Steve heard a sudden wind and thunder came upon the garden. "Oh, they did not eat the wrong fruit, did they?" said Steve as he noticed the sound of disobedience.

As Adam and Eve were covering themselves, realizing that they were naked, Steve hurried off to find them. Then as the serpent appeared and asked, "Steve, care to join me for what you want?"

"Not on your life, snake dude!" Steve told the serpent. For he would not put his trust in that evil reptile. And so he turned away.

The moment Adam and Eve hid themselves, the Lord called out to the man. "Adam, where are you?" He asked.

"I heard you in the garden," Adam answered. "I was afraid because I was naked. So I hid!"

"Who told you that you were naked?" the Lord asked. "Have you eaten the fruit of the tree I commanded you not to eat?"

"The woman you put here with me!" Adam explained. "She gave me some fruit from the tree, and I ate it!"

Then God asked Eve, "What have you done?"

"The serpent is the one who tricked me!" explained Eve. "And that's why I ate the fruit!" So the Lord cursed on the serpent, explaining that the sinful life will come. As punishment for Adam and Eve, the Lord cast them out of the Garden of Eden.

"Hey you guys! Wait up!" Steve called when he found Adam and Eve. Steve followed them out; then, they were driven out of the garden. As they walked, Steve looked back and saw something blazing up in the air with a won-drous sight—a great flaming sword that God had placed in the garden, guarding the way to the tree of life.

Steve felt so sorry for what Adam and Eve had done. For they had lost Eden forever. "Well, some special listeners they turned out to be," said Steve to himself. "Guess that makes them disobedient to God, and so am I sometimes." Then on the journey alone he goes, as his first life adventure continues in the Bible times.

NOAH'S ARK

Genesis
Chapter 6

After leaving the Garden of Eden, Steve discovered a huge ark. There, he met Noah and his family. He was told by God to build the ark because there will be a flood to destroy evil man kind in the entire earth. "You're here to make fun of us like our neighbors or to help us build the ark?" Noah asked. "There's not a lot of time before the Lord brings the flood. We have a lot of work to do. You are welcome to help."

"Well, I don't see why not." Steve smiled and said, "Guess I'll be glad to help, just as long I don't get a splinter."

So Steve helped Noah, his wife, and their family. It will take some time and hard work to build the ark. "Man if only I had work gloves for this job!" said Steve to himself as he was helping carry some heavy wood. It may not be fun for him, but it was the right thing to do with Noah and his family.

Finally the ark was finished. Noah did what the Lord commanded him to do. He and his family, including Steve, entered on board. Even all the animals have now come to the ark. The birds, the beasts, and creepy things, male and female, two by two. "Wow! Now this is what I like to call Zoo Cruise!" said Steve when all the animals came on board and took their places.

So Noah made sure everyone was ready on board. Then as God closed the door of the ark, the mighty thunder roared. The rain finally came, and the great flood lifted the ark above as it began to float upon the waters that rose higher and higher upon the face of the earth until it was covered forty-five feet high above the mountains. "Whoa...all hands on deck, dudes!" shouted Steve as he felt the ark shake. As it was raining for forty days and forty nights, everything on earth was destroyed. For only Noah, his family, the animals, and Steve remained lucky to be alive.

After forty days and forty nights, the rain stopped. They remained on board for another 150 days. Steve was very bored. He stayed busy by helping to feed the animals and exercising like push-ups and jumping jacks. Even two of the monkeys were copying his jumping moves. "Hey, am I a monkey coach to you guys?" said Steve.

Stepping outside the deck of the ark, Steve looked around, gazing at the entire clear ocean. Still no land, only water, Steve saw dolphins jumping and splashing around. "Flood, flood, flood over the sea!" said Steve to himself. "If this boat were my house, I would spend my whole life on this ocean cruise. If only there's a bathroom here."

So then Noah sent out the raven to find land and come back. Unable to find the dry land, he soon sent out a dove, but he came back with no luck. After seven days, Steve said with a yawn, "Whoa, oh, man! How long is this gonna be! Seriously." Then again, Noah let a dove out the second time and said to Steve as he said to his family, "Have faith as I have faith. There will soon be land out there, while we must wait on the ark. No matter how long it will take, we can always trust in God. For we are meant to be special to him." And soon, the dove came back with a green olive twig in its beak. For it was a sign that there is land that the dove finally found.

And so, when Noah sent out the dove one last time, he never returned. Noah looked and saw the earth was dry. For after another seven days, the ark had come to rest on the mountain of Ararat. God opened the door and told Noah to leave the ark. "Come, everyone! shouted Noah with joy. "Let's all go forth from the ark!" He went forth along with his sons, his wife, and his son's wives. All the animals and birds, two by two, went out with them, including Steve.

"Yeah! This feel's good to be back on the perfect dry land!" said Steve, stretching his legs after a very long boat ride for many days.

As everyone was out of the ark, God blessed Noah and his sons and said to them, "Be fruitful and multiply. May you have children and grandchildren. Even all the animals and birds. Fill the earth and rule over it." Then God sent a rainbow as a sign of a promise that He will never again destroy the earth by sending a flood.

As Noah and his family praised the Lord, Noah's wife gave a bag of food to Steve as he was preparing to continue his trip. "Farewell, Steve," said Noah. "As you were the only special helper that my family and I could thank since the day before the great flood. And now, may the Lord bless you on your journey."

"Well, it sure was worth it in the end anyway!" said Steve. "So you're welcome! After all, I am autistic. 'Bye now!" Then on a journey alone he goes.

THE TOWER OF BABEL

Genesis
Chapter 11

After a time of a long boat ride with Noah during the great flood, Steve walked toward Shinar and discovered a big, tall, gigantic Tower of Babel. "Wow, that's the tallest tower I have ever seen in my whole life!" said Steve, with the amazingly sight. Staring up to the very top reaching the sky above the clouds, it was being built by a whole group of men who thought they could reach heaven.

But since it was glorifying themselves, that's when God punished them by confusing them with each of their own different languages. They were unable to finish building the tower since everyone else kept arguing as they could not understand each other. Neither does Steve understand them as he heard them yelling with their funny different languages nearby and said with a laugh as he walked by, around the tower, "Ha, ha! And so this is where it all started! The whole bunch of different people with funny different languages, who built a great, tall, heavenly tower and called it Babel, and I'm the only one that's autistic who speaks English! Huh! And I thought their speech got no sense of humor." Then on the journey alone, he continues to go.

Genesis

Chapter 21

After a few miles from there, as nightfall began, Steve walked over to Beersheba where he met a young boy named Isaac near the village. "Evening there, kid!" said Steve. "Whatcha doing in the middle of the night?"

"I'm using my abacus that my father gave me to count all the stars in the sky!" said Isaac.

"Really?" Steve wondered. "Nothing makes you sleepy like when you count a million, thousands of them? I mean, that's a whole lot a stars up there!"

"That's how many descendants that will be for my father and me!" said Isaac, and he led Steve to his father Abraham.

"Isaac! My beloved son!" called Abraham. "And who might you be, traveler?"

"I'm Steve!" said Steve. "The autistic traveler!" Abraham welcomed Steve for supper and to stay for the night. He shared with him the story about the time before Isaac was born when three angel travelers came to Abraham that day. And the men told him that he and his wife Sarah will have a son. Hearing behind the tent door, Sarah laughed to herself.

Then God asked, "Why did Sarah laugh? Is it because she's too old to have a child? As I promised, next year, you shall have a son."

"And that's why I called him Isaac, which means laughter," said Abraham as his story ended.

Then later that day, God said to Abraham for what he decided to test his faith and obedience, "Take your son Isaac, your only beloved one, and go to the land of Moriah. Give him to me as an offering on a mountain that I will show you in honor of me."

"Offering... my son Isaac?" Abraham said with shock. And even though God's words were heartbreaking, he knew that he had to obey, so the next morning, Abraham got up early and asked Isaac to come with him. They split each of their wood for the offering and were off to a place God told him. When Steve woke up, he saw them go by.

"Could it be a call from God for a sacrifice?" Steve guessed. Wondering, he followed them slowly farther to take a peek without being noticed.

As they arrived at the top of the mountain spot where God had asked, Isaac said to Abraham, "Well, we have the wood, Father, but where's the lamb for the offering?"

"God will provide the lamb for the offering my son," said Abraham. Steve hid behind the boulder and spied on them as Abraham built an altar and laid out the wood. Then he tied up Isaac and put him on the altar as he was about to sacrifice his own son.

But then God called out, "Abraham! Don't lay a hand on the boy! For now I know you are willing to trust and obey me." Then, Abraham saw a ram caught in the thicket by its horns and offered it to God instead of his son.

"Like different father, like special son," Steve whispered to himself, for he knew it was a test. Then on a journey alone, he continues.

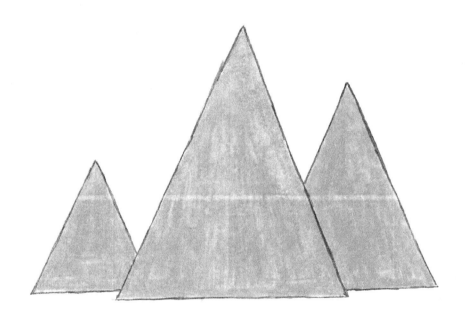

JOSEPH AND HIS BROTHERS

Genesis

Chapter 36

And so, after the time of Abraham, Steve traveled to the land of Egypt as he discovered the ancient city. "Wow! Egypt!" said Steve, staring at the city with the incredible sight. "Home of the ancient Pharaohs! I heard this place is nothing but trouble and torture." Curiously, Steve walked over to see what Egypt was like, where all the traveling crowd were walking to the entrance for the harvest.

When Steve entered, exploring the city of Egypt, as he looked at something pretty and wondrous, Steve accidentally bumped into and met Joseph the governor of Egypt. "Oh, uh, excuse me, sir!" said Steve respectfully as he felt embarrassed "I mean, your honor! Really sorry about that!

"Oh no, it's all right! No need to worry!" said Joseph kindly.

"I'm Joseph, in charge of the harvest in Egypt. What's your name?"

"I'm Steve," Steve said. "I'm autistic, which means of course either special or different. Mostly different, I travel alone."

"Well, now you interest me," Joseph said. "You're welcome to be my guest."

As Joseph welcomed Steve, he shared with him a backstory of how his special and different life had been on that simple and difficult time. Joseph was telling Steve about how he ended up living in Egypt after living in Canaan with his father, Jacob, who loved him so, more than he loved his other sons, who were mean and jealous of him. For he told his father and brothers about the dream he had about the sun, the moon, and eleven stars that were bowing down to him. So as a favorite son, Jacob gave him a magnificent and most colorful coat as Joseph wore it with joy. And now his brothers hated him more; they tackled him and sold him into slavery. Lying to Jacob, they put lamb's blood on Joseph's coat, explaining he was killed by a wild animal and made Jacob feel heartbroken in sorrow.

The next thing Joseph told Steve about was when he was first brought into Egypt as a slave; he was then sent to prison for no reason. Then, two years later, Joseph was sent to the king of Egypt, for he was troubled about the dreams he had, and what Joseph told the king, by the spirit of God, was to prepare for a famine that would come to pass for seven years. "And that's how I became the governor of Egypt," said Joseph. "God always provided a way for me as he does for all the people."

"Well, isn't that an interesting story!" said Steve, lying comfy, wearing an Egyptian wig while snacking. "You know that part in the beginning of the story, about the coat of many colors your dad gave you? That would be so cool if I have one of those to wear... for autism."

So later that day, Steve helped Joseph pour out and give away some grain to the hungry people at the storehouse. Then Joseph spotted his brothers. When they came to him and bowed down to their knees, Joseph glared at them, saying, "You men are spies! Aren't you?"

"Oh no, my Lord, we are not spies!" they said, for they did not know it was Joseph. "We are the family of twelve brothers, one is dead, the other is the youngest who's with our father at home."

"We'll see if that's true or not!" Joseph said. "Come back when you bring your youngest brother to me. If not, you shall be put to death!" Joseph turned away and cried as they left, and Steve noticed when he heard them.

"So those must be the mean brothers, huh?" said Steve to himself. "Boy are they gonna get it."

The brothers knew they had been punished by God for what they have done to Joseph in the first place. So when they arrived home in Canaan, they told Jacob what happened, "Father! The governor of Egypt treated us like we are spies! And the only way that he will believe that we are not is we must take Benjamin to Egypt!"

But Jacob shook his head sadly and said, "My beloved Joseph is gone, and now you want to take Benjamin!? No!" Then as the famine grew worse, the food that the brothers brought from Egypt were running out. When Jacob asked his sons to go back and buy some more, they could not go unless they take Benjamin with them. "If that's what we must do, then go." Jacob agreed.

"Don't worry, Father! I'll be all right!" Benjamin said, and off they left for Egypt.

As the brothers arrived at the palace, Joseph ordered the servants to make them food. As the brothers were seated, eating and drinking, Joseph made sure Benjamin got plenty to eat. Even Steve had plenty to eat for lunch also. "Hm, I wonder how this turns out to be with these brother dudes," said Steve, watching them. As Joseph figured out a plan, a test to find out if the brothers had changed, he ordered his servants to fill their grain sacks and put his silver cup in the sack of the youngest.

The next morning, the brothers were sent away. But as they were leaving the city, Joseph sent the guards after them and searched through each of their sacks. They found a silver cup in Benjamin's sack. Back to the palace they were taken to Joseph, where he said to them, "The one who had stolen the cup will be my slave! The rest of you may go home!"

"Please, sir!" one of the men begged. "Let Benjamin go! Our Father will die in heartbreak if he loses him, for he already lost one whom he loved so! Take one of us instead!"

The brothers had finally changed, and Joseph said who he was. "I am your brother Joseph whom you sold into Egypt. But it was only God who sent me here to save your lives. Now go to my father and bring him here. With all your family, so we will all live in Egypt!" With joy and forgiving, both Joseph and Benjamin hugged each other with tears.

"One big happy brotherhood family," said Steve, watching happily for them.

And so at last, Jacob's whole family of seventy men, women, and children had arrived from Canaan to Egypt. Steve hopped along with Joseph into the chariot and raced out to meet Jacob. Very excitingly, Joseph went before his father and threw his arms around him, crying to his father as Steve was amazed of what a big family it was, knowing how special Joseph was meant to be, blessed by God as a visionary. Steve was ready to go as he went up the sandhill, waving good-bye to them. "Nice happy family reunion, but boy do I have a long way to go! I mean, hey! I am the lone autistic traveler you know! 'Bye now!" Then on the journey alone he went.

About the Author

Steven Tomasino loves the bible and its stories. Diagnosed autistic at **4** years old, he learned to speak using phrases from movies that he loved to watch. He loves to draw and create his own ideas of bible characters, among others. He lives in Texas, with his mom, step-dad, and brothers. They are all members of First Baptist Church of Castroville. God has blessed Steven with a love for His Word and with a talent for drawing to express his love. Although Steven struggles with some of the typical disadvantages and hardships that autism brings, he is happy and healthy, loves to help around the house, and loves to share his drawings and stories with anyone interested. It has been his dream to create a book of his drawings. We thank God that He has made it possible.